COVENTRY SCHOOLS'
LIBRARY SERVICE

Please return this book on or before last
date stamped.

D0419315

COVENTRY SCHOOLS LIBRARY SERVICE	
16-Oct-2008	JF
PETERS	

the Dudgeon is coming

Lynley Dodd

PUFFIN

'Pass on the news,'
said the bombazine bear
to the taffeta cat
who was dressing her hair,
'The Dudgeon is coming,
he's shy
and polite . . .

'Look after the Dudgeon –
he's coming
tonight.'

'Pass on the news,'
   said the taffeta cat
   to the hopalong snoot
   in a ten-gallon hat,
'The Dudgeon is coming!
   He isn't polite . . .

'Look out for the Dudgeon –
he's coming
tonight!'

'Pass on the news,'
  said the hopalong snoot
  to the blue cockatoo
  who was knitting a suit,
'The Dudgeon is coming!
  He'll give you a fright . . .

'Stay clear of the Dudgeon —
he's coming
tonight!'

'Pass on the news,'
said the stickleback twitch
to the pineapple pig
in her mudwallow ditch,
'The Dudgeon is coming!
There might be a fight . . .

'Beware of the Dudgeon –
he's coming
TONIGHT!'

'Pass on the news,'
    said the pineapple pig
    to the omnibus owl
    in his Regency wig,
'Warn everybody
    with all of your might . . .

'THE TERRIBLE DUDGEON
IS COMING
TONIGHT!'

Then came a swish
and a shiver of leaves,
a soft pitter-pat
through the shadowy trees.
A very small voice – like a bumblebee hum – said . . .

'Hi,
I'm the Dudgeon.
I've finally
come!'

PUFFIN BOOKS

Published by the Penguin Group: London, New York, Australia,
Canada, India, Ireland, New Zealand and South Africa
Penguin Books Ltd, Registered Offices: 80 Strand, London WC2R 0RL, England

puffinbooks.com

First published in New Zealand by Mallinson Rendel Publishers Ltd 2008
First published in Great Britain in Puffin Books 2008
1 3 5 7 9 10 8 6 4 2
Copyright © Lynley Dodd, 2008
All rights reserved
The moral right of the author/illustrator has been asserted
Printed and bound in China through Colorcraft Ltd., Hong Kong
ISBN: 978-0-141-38467-2